James E. Krendel-Clark's

I0520685

Hitman

(a récit)

Hitman (a récit) © 2022 Orbis Tertius Press

Cover image adapted from @nahelabdlhadi

Cover design and interior layout by Kimberley Palsat

ISBN: 978-1-7781566-0-1

Orbis Tertius Press

for Edward Gorey

male (adjective)

1 a (1) : of, relating to, or being the sex that typically has the capacity to produce relatively small, usually motile gametes which fertilize the eggs of a female

   (2) : having or producing only stamens or staminate flowers // a *male* holly

  b: having a gender identity that is the opposite of female

  c: made up of usually adult members of the male sex: consisting of males // a *male* choir

  d: characteristic of boys, men, or the male sex : exhibiting maleness // a deep *male* voice

  e: designed for or typically used by boys or men // a *male* cologne // *male* contraceptives

  f: engaged in or exercised by boys or men // A social code that taught women deference to *male* power in return for protection was upended ... –Jane E. Schultz

  g: having a quality (such as vigor or boldness) sometimes associated with the male sex

2 : MASCULINE sense 3a // a *male* rhyme

3: designed with a projecting part for fitting into a corresponding female part // a *male* hose coupling

-Merriam-Webster Online Dictionary

1.

"**I** hate it when stuff annoys me," said an austere cybergothicdyke in a gratingly nasal valley-girl flourish of phlegmbitters. "I'm going to write a manifesto, and I'll call it 'Against Annoyance'." "That'll show 'em," chimed her subby gaybestfriend, hands in corduroys, smarmy. The goth chick said nothing and scowled. Darby Frown, as he strolled past them, swam in and out of identifying with this stoned e-girl's mushmouth ramblings and his own inner monologue. The labyrinth that was his life was crystallizing into something that might be manageable, navigable, albeit transitory and sinister, puzzling. The map was in hand, and the end was in sight. This was the life of a grizzled hitman. Take no prisoners attitude. Simulation or no simulation.

The trail of schizophrenic scribblings that constituted Darby's œuvre, up to this point, were finally leading somewhere, somewhere coherent, somewhere into something like a narrative, like a biography. At least loosely speaking. He envisioned a sort of metafiction framework to contain the performances that added up to a life that belonged to him, basically. But all abstract frippery aside, his main job, killing people for money, kept him supplied with the fundamental trappings of a financially stable and independent lifestyle. It also gave him a hardcore edge that scared people who saw him walking down the street, hands balled up into fists (they were *relaxed* fists, which was what made him seem even more threatening, like a poised martial artist; when he let his hands relax, fingers pointing down, opposite hand moving with opposite leg in a coordinated shuffling gait, a physiognomy that had the hollowness and austerity of a Chinese scholar's rock, he looked even more frightening, because nothing was hidden), leather jacket encasing him in sleek animality, fashion passion. An increasingly coherent path was forming in his mind, like a crawler algorithm scripted from termite data, carnivorously inevitable, the coagulation of his destiny, an oracle for his *existenz*, if you will. As he disposed of corpses, he felt things crystallizing.

Everything up to this point had been nothing but chaotic scrying, scrambling up scree to divine a secret way up the mountain, a mere game, for Darby. No more superstition now, though. Just focus. Focus. Focus. Focus. Zeroing in... At home, he drained the blood from an arm and wrapped it carefully, ritualistically, in cheesecloth, tied-off with twine, into the freezer-safe, the frozen vault, later to be hurled into the sea during a lightning storm, after saying a prayer to Poseidon, the sea-lord, but not before using the arm for various photographic experiments and collage (Darby found the work of Hans Bellmer inspiring; he was also an avid Rauschenberg addict). It was part of his creative process, and it was as if this process had finally exhausted itself, leaving no other option but to advance, relying only on the most delicate filament of intuition, a phoenix grouchily gaping its madman's face from out of the ashes of burnout. Darby ceased fearing that he might be a petit-bourgeois dilettante; there was a quiet confidence to his demeanor, he was a genuine artist, a real pro. Darby hated self-help books, he saw them as fascist, promoting virulent narcissism. 'Mein Kampf' was the first self-help book, and he hated Hitler. Darby was one of those "new" Nietzscheans who was quick to defend N against his fascist appropriation by that scumbag sister of his, Elisabeth Förster, wife of Bernhard Förster, who called the Jews "a parasite on the German body," and started an Aryan cult in Paraguay, only to burn out and, ironically, die by suicide the same year as Nietzsche went insane. Surely Nietzsche's madness was precipitated in part by the passionate interest taken by a handful of anti-Semites in Nietzsche's work (Nietzsche who was practically embarrassed to be German and referred to his sister as "a vengeful, anti-Semitic goose"), even during his own lifetime. But in the end it was much more Wagner (Wagner, who, towards the end of their friendship, inspired, quite literally, fits of vomiting in Nietzsche) who inspired Hitler. Darby cleaned his gun, methodically as he contemplated this frustrating nexus of questions about Nietzsche and Nationalism, listening to a recording of shakuhachi flute improvisations.

The terrifying night of youth was finally over, and love made more sense, love in all its abyssal, sinuous depth was no longer the threatening reptile that had once tattooed the folds of his brain with its sinister topology. No, he had evolved beyond that. The scarification remained, but he was expanding. He knew what he wanted. Fear had finally left him, deserted him, even. Let bygones be bygones, he thought to himself. "From now on I shall pray for my enemies, like a religious person, like someone who believes in Santa Claus." He didn't believe in Santa Claus, but he could pretend. He wavered a little on this point. He thought he understood the principle of loving one's enemies. But on the other hand, he felt that he had to forgive himself for hating or harming, whenever he would hate or harm, which he often did. That made sense. He needed to have a consistent ethical code. Or did he? He squinted, profoundly. He thought about how he had killed Rex Orifice, the irritating art critic. Stabbed him right in the glottis and watched him gurgle. That had been very pleasurable. *Very* pleasurable. Fitting that an arch-gargoyle of the cultural ivory tower should end with a gurgle, his eloquence cancelled in crushed vocal-chords. Rex should have known not to get so addicted to gambling. Then he wouldn't have racked up such massive mob debt. He should have known. Well, now he's six feet deep. Darby Frown, consummate hitman, crossed himself ineptly, then caught himself halfway and stopped. "Damn it," he mumbled, in a haze of confusion. "No more superstition. Fucking get rational."

Get Rational was the title of a self-help book he was reading. It was the only book he'd touched for the past 7 months. This reading withdrawal was part of a dopamine fast he was riding out. He looked up at the enormous crucifix that hung in the living room, above the television set, and smiled, murkily. Even though he no longer believed, he was sure that Jesus Christ, man-messiah, agreed with him.

A smell of mystic lavender suffused Darby's cold ghost as the floorboards creaked. A phantasmagoria of disconnected but weirdly linked ideas floated through his mind as the lights on the wifi router flashed suggestively. Darby's sinuses ached. Tiny ants crawled over his desk. Doors swung on their hinges, and outside, branches swung wildly in the screaming wind. Locked in a cataleptic stupor, Darby sipped coffee from a mug decorated with tiny golden alligators. They seemed to wink at him, effusively. Feeling the interior of his molars with his reptile tongue. {*Always deft, never inept, always deft, never inept.*} That was his mantra for the day. He skipped ahead in *Get Rational* to see what the next day's mantra was. You could stop a bullet with that book. It wasn't just some nazified "might is right" self-help bullshit, it was in fact a kind of dadaist parody of self-help literature written by a famous artist, and it actually worked! The best cults are ironic cults.

The new mantra was: *"Zero in and move out, zero in and move out."* Sweet. The taste of haste. The dysphoria of a lightning bolt squinting down a walk, leaving his body, furrowed lips, irises shrinking and dilating in a dynamic blurring of the existential lens. With a subtle flourish, Darby pulled-shut the squeaking door to his spooky study.

Darby had once seen a movie in which a paranoid schizophrenic tried to cut government implants out of his skull. Darby wasn't paranoid, but he could imagine pretending to be. He chewed on the arm of his plastic glasses. He stroked the beard on his chin. As he reflected, an owl hooted, somewhere off in the soft distance. No, it wasn't in the distance, it was extremely close. No, it was in the distance again. Strange. The night plays tricks on the mind. So does the day. Strange. Maybe it was the owl-shaped clock on his wall, but it only hooted on the hour, and it was 17 past. There was also a tiny metal statue of an owl behind and to the left of Darby's laptop, an inch or so away from his SEAGATE external hard drive.

Statues cannot speak. Frowning, Frown fiddled with the statue and then folded his fingers in concentration, brooding over a lost universe. He was beginning to realize that the internet was not nearly as fascinating and miraculous as it had once seemed, in the early days. Nor as fast. Should he phone his I.S.P., go for an upgrade? No, not worth the trouble. Fuck it. Just fuck it. The potential people saw in the web for political organization was an illusion. Frown knew that. After all, a cold-blooded professional killer develops a certain cynical sense for the hard reality of it all. Darby was an artist, but he was an assassin first. He was a professional, he was a man who could stick to the plan. *"No stains on my soul, I'm whole as a ghoul / No stains on my soul..."* Darby caught himself repeating the mantra from two weeks ago.

2.

𝔇arby fiddled with the little metal owl, a paperweight of sorts, and set it down in exactly the same position it had previously been in on his desk. It was 12:35 AM. Chewing compulsively on his fat lips, Darby started to use the new mantra with no uncertain fury. *"Zero in and move out, zero in and move out,"* he mumbled several times before he internalized it and repeated it silently. He stared with blind rage at a poster of Duchamp's moustachioed Mona Lisa, and then at the poster to the immediate right of that, an Op Art thing, sort of an optical illusion by Victor Vasarely called *Gestalt 4*. This visual stimulus made Darby feel crazed, and his eyes began to bug out in bubbling arousal. He tried to focus inward. As stated in the 3rd volume of *Get Rational*, the goal was to picture a tiny person perched on a chair in the center of your head mouthing the mantra like a creepy ghost, with the saucy confidence of a talk-show guest but the scary evil of a living doll, somehow fusing those disparate qualities into one little inner homunculus. *Get Rational* called this "the superduperego." A paradoxical consciousness, befitting a psychonaut.

Darby's tics were an epileptic arrogance, a furiously restless need to transgress the organic boundaries of who he was, letting the electricity of his ailment poke out into the outside of tender, networked awkwardness… like poking a glowing-hot needle into the chafed skin of every hyper-sensitive ghost in his peripheral awareness. The Youtube generated playlist of "rock music" that he was listening to switched over to one of his favourite David Bowie songs. Youtube had done a good job with this algorithm: '5.15 Angels Have Gone' off of *Heathen*. Bowie clearly understood the profoundly interesting depression that befalls the creative sort. Darby sipped his cold coffee, grimly, feeling every aching twinge of sore, burnt-out muscle fiber. He recalled the grudging way his father had conceded that the two of them were "different," earlier, on the phone. Parental resentment, entanglements exit the grizzly bottom of jungle triads, neurons geared for deadly anal buzz. He pulled pensively at his soul-patch. Honestly, things were going extremely well.

As Darby pulled wispily at the gruff beard fuzz, he was startled suddenly by a sense of ghostly apparition on his left side, but quickly pulled himself together, back into himself. Indifferent to ghosts. Get rational. Push away any and all distractions. Peel-back the pressure points. Focus. The thorny problem the ghosts presented was not interesting to Darby. *Brain phantoms*, as they used to say. Darby pinched his nose reflectively. Back when reading was considered to be an addiction, maybe even a sin, the gothic novel was invented. Darby slid his glasses arm up and down his forehead, thoughtfully, letting the spectacles dangle like the loosely pretentious gesture of a spry dandy. He contracted his face into a narrow, pointy look.

Catching his own reflection in the mirror, he considers that he looks like Jacques Derrida. He doesn't like the comparison. Tom Waits is playing on the iPhone, plugged to earbuds, rattling tympanum rust. Knitting his eyebrows and grimly gritting his cigarette and grinding his teeth, he grimaces at the abnormality of institutionalized inequality. Minuscule movements of the face, twistedmouth. The blues ain't nothing but a lyrical expression of the catastrophe. Primate grimace.

3.

The porno didn't do it anymore. He didn't get hard alone. He was just waiting to matriculate so he could smash up on the cute fellow grad-students. Yes, Darby was going for a PhD, in linguistics. Strange how the world works. A man whose hands are deadly weapons chooses to pursue the intellectual life. But nothing pays the bills like being a professional assassin. Darby had grown so confident in his power that he abhorred women. The last girlfriend he'd had had left him for a famous rapper. Her loss. Given how small the graduate program at Duke is, maybe he'd have to resort to the dating apps he reviles to meet anybody, the PhD program being positively infiltrated by dykish feminists. Lately the only thing that gave him a hard-on was food. Life feels like a cartoon. A nightmare. But Darby was a professional. Nobody fucked with him. "Don't think twice, cold as ice. Don't think twice, cold as ice. Don't think twice…"

He was sick of collecting anime action figures and looking for a new hobby. That self-care shit gave him a headache. Sculpture, he'd tried. Collage, sure. At the end of the day, he fell apart like a quivering wreck, like human jello, a moistly limp, limply moist burnout, wet towel applied to mouldering embers… when he wasn't pointing a loaded gun at the head of someone who had crossed the organized crime group he worked for. But this vulnerability was irrelevant, since it never interfered with him pulling the trigger when he had to. He inhaled the radioactive serenity of the internet like a spirit medium. His new PRADA jacket empowered him slightly, sure. A skull and cross-bones tattoo adorned his upper arm. Beside the jolly roger there was a symbol for saturn, which was a brand, as opposed to a tattoo. Darby was trying to learn how to work on cars. A tailpipe from a truck he'd refurbished lay against the side of his bookshelf. His library was eclectic. Hobbies abounded. People looked up to him.

Frown was a polymath, but he was insecure about it. He was at heart one of those punk motherfuckers that people like to dismiss as narcissistic.

He lived in the mirrorplay of his own genius. It was a vibrating coil, an electromagnet, gravitational. Pre-seizure aura, permanent. Auto-hypnotic clairvoyance. Sinister. Frown whipped a butterfly knife out of one of his desk drawers and flipped it around maniacally, in dazzling patterns, the polished surfaces of the knife sending reflections from the hot halogen bulbs that lit the room, dancing on the walls and ceiling. Back when he was a surly hooligan, as a kid, he would impress his buddies with these nifty and nutty tricks. Now it was simply a way of relieving stress. This and the treadmill kept him fit and lucid, no flab. He threw the knife "deftly" at a poster of Richard Nixon. Right between the eyes. He hated Nixon. God DAMN it did he hate Nixon. Fucking scumbag. You have to pick who you hate with extreme care. Nixon was the perfect symbolic nemesis for some obscure reason. This way Darby could sublimate anger strategically. He lit up a cigar. His gravity rolled the planets of his eyes and spun the chorus of his strummed veins like a distorted echoing intercom directly to his bones. The noise that in them rang was vox gen y, a generational song that could be sung for all, like Walt Whitman, yeah. Yeah. He wrote that one down. Reaching towards a bowl of fruit on his coffee table, he hesitated between pear and orange. Orange. He took the peel off in one spiraling rind all of a piece.

He thought that to be a polymath you had to be a genius, and sometimes he worried he wasn't really enough of a genius in the Nietzschean sense, just an imposter playing the part of one, poorly, like a con artist, at best a secret agent. Maybe he was more of a genius à la Kierkegaard, a man of the moment. He liked that one. 'Horse Rotovator' by Coil was playing in the background. It was 3:33 AM, his favourite time of day. More often than not, Darby avoided sleep, partly by snorting vyvanse and partly just by being totally crazed all of the time. Earlier that day, Darby had learned that people in low income brackets and especially immigrants had a statistically higher likelihood of becoming clinically paranoid. He assumed this was also true of the loser zvrzh_G™-heads who hung around the compound alleyways {{zvrzh_G™, drug of the future}}. He tried to avoid them but they'd hoodwink him into another poker game, always when he was too drunk to care. They met in a back room at the famous gay club, SUPEREGO. SUPEREGO was famous for its stylish orgies, but Darby just came to gamble. A lot of underworld top-brass would turn up for these all-night no-holds-barred poker games. "Care for a foot massage?" the robots would whimper (as Darby wended his way through the chaos of the club to get to the room where the game was held). They asked this question cryptically, with a self-flagellating, masochistic aura. Was it a hallucination? Hideous hallucinatory stench, this. He threw up a little in his mouth, and swallowed it back down. Gross. The freakazoids with all the clown makeup tittered and giggled. He'd usually win at poker, especially at a time like this with a portentous cancer moon, but he hated that he had to put up with the obnoxious attempts on the part of these sly society-types to be interesting and unique, these robotic chiptuned hipstercoils, urgh how he hated them. Irrational anger, nothing to do with their sexuality, just weird hate.

The crystal thousand dollar etched chip he held in his pocket for good luck had symbols on it that spoke of a poker prophecy. One day a gambling messiah would free the repressed masses from their baroque chrysalis casings and open a new cultural center designed by the world's leading architect.

4.

One thing Darby had noticed, to his immense irritation, was that zvrzh_G™ addicts seemed desperate to be seen, they developed all kinds of strange tics and eccentricities, even manufactured misfortunes out of pure karmic fluid to get your attention {this *is* working, isn't it?}. They constantly uploaded videos to Vrumio and Spune. Darby pretended not to pay attention. But it was hard. They were just so outrageously flamboyant, and so vibrantly in your face, clucking their tongues and snapping their fingers, which were surgically elongated. Later he would record everything in his crisp, cute sparkly journal he'd bought at WalMart. Sure, sometimes he gave in to the glitter and the razzmatazz, adding to his collection of chintzy camp schlock. But you could tell he was tough as nails, and definitely didn't fit in with this fruity crowd. He was a fucking hitman, and he contained profundities, after all, and it showed, enough to put some dogs on edge, and fascinate young children and the young at heart. Sometimes he would throw them a bone and flash his million dollar smile, teeth sharp as knives and surgically elongated. Other times he was as opaque and distant as a slab of marble.

5.

Fey Shen, nipples cauterized, drooled like a slorgslarve, possibly a gluetroll or a void-larva, slorping down pu erh tea like a sleepy broodgollum. Oh, the ailments of the throat and lungs!! Always a crusty grease_goblinx. Sure, he'd seen some colourful vistas of characters hanging around the prison section of the complex_all_around_enclosure. The complex was a diverse clustered+cluster+enclosure of villages sequestered in clawdance//vibratime//ultra_tutelage// within the walls of prison inside of church inside of mall, on top of hill, a spiral_spiral_spiral_etc ssmooth ass mucousss, intestinally nesssted. Shady crooks in drag, as fanatical as nazis fuck each other in the ass in the slimy, vermin-ridden, sewagecrooked corridors of the impossible castlevortex. All in of it melted glue. And inside of it all, sure, snxrled, all matter of sin and trash with the vortextwisted horrorhumor whirled and rattlejizzled around in the blinding air_molecules, impregnating grotesque DNA in your veins with shards of plutonium, the air hot with a stench that could derange all the senses, like the viral_fetid center of an expensive vintage wine's foamy black bouquet (but this ain't no madeleine, it's government_mandated ambient odour and the delirium it induces is enforced by syringe-wielding mindcops dressed in their hilarious frippery, grotesque goretex folds of runwaystyled jackets with swarowskicrystalled runes and faces foul as Alfred Kubin's most lucid and distorted nightmares, symmetrical bindi rorschach, eyes swastikacancelled), a halloween purityparty with Frankenstein's randy bride, symmetricalfascist musclerelaxed g.o.a.t. poppers you're dressed as Darth Vader, twisted doublehelix history books about the great war --> and a set of false eyelashes like your girlfriend likes to wear. Novelty contact lenses etcetera, dysmorphic fingernails. Meaning breaks down as performative statements invade you with sybilline energy, elusive yet invasive, yet somehow reminiscent of a blockbuster film about mutant x people {I'm not going to say "x men" that's sexist}. "I feel like an indebted man," thought Darby, in between recitations of his mantra {{*"go, implode, go, implode, go, implode, go, implode, etc."*}}. Grenades pop off somewhere else in the maze, or maybe fireworks. Splitting headache.

Get Rational {which, by the way, was written by reality TV star and religious guru Sven Grendel, a very charismatic and hyperintelligent man, in this case it is appropriate to say "man" since that's how he chooses to identify, however outré it may be} says that to be a slave to Grod is key to the krell {{krell is ovipositor like sci-fi classic forbidden planet, humanoid imposter syndrome vortex very tasty}}. It's important to say "Grod" instead of "God," because there is no such thing as God. That way you're still being very very rational. "I know I'm extremely fictional, but my textuality is coded in gestures of graphic design with a focus on branding, the iconicity and all that Rem Koolhaas jazz, yadda yadda, so on and so forth, on the contemporary city, etcetera, its deliriousness and what have you and so on and so on. You know that feeling clustered around a campfire? Yeah, like cowboys, boytoy but less rustic like nordic viking brood. Cavemen transitioning from raw to cooked or upgrading software to the next version. I'm still a hillbilly, in other words, but I know how to code. Seriously, I promise, I really know how to code. I mean, I'm no Steve Jobs but I get by. Picture *Hackers* meets *War Games* meets *Demon Seed* meets *Videodrome*, that's my total vibe, my aesthetic." Darby realized that he was lisping this incoherent speech to a flexicrack rap junky lurched against a sloping brick wallsurface. What the fuck was going on. *"Go, implode, go implode,"* he muttered {{his mantra barely edging out the intrusive OCD thought: "vortexfuck suckvortex fuckvortex suck suck vortex"; according to the author of *Get Rational* this was normal brain noise and meant to be ignored; still, it was an amazing coincidence that the example of brain noise given in *Get Rational* was the exact brain noise that Darby experienced on a regular basis, and this was part of his reason for adhering so rigidly to the book; "thoughts of fuckvortexes and suck-vortexes are to be ignored," those were the exact words; amazing! prophetic!}}, shuffling off this mortal coil. With frayed leather jacket half on, nude left arm riddled with track-marks covered in tattoos. {{{Now I learn what it means to be me. Rule number 1 from *Get Rational*: "have low self-esteem, will not travel. Have *high* self esteem, you're good to go." Sure. I feel like the inventor of a new layer of hell. I'm stoned but I've gotten tired of eating these chips, almost. It's 6:57 PM and I'm sliding into the listless first person. I've lost track of calendrical time. Normally I would feel jaded about this, but I had an epiphany last night and everything feels new. I don't exactly remember the contents of the epiphany...}}} Darby was crouched atop the Potential Center, his calf muscles twitching with laser-focused athleticism, his quads surging with power, with all the dynamism of a comic-strip superhero, pointing his sniper rifle over at the Pray Center, where Coral Problem, a famous elf politician, was eating at the new Zorb Portal restaurant {Zorb Portal, the famous chef, who, as it happens, was also an elf; rumours of an elven conspiracy against the Maserati family were confirmed and it was Darby's job to take out their most powerful leader}. {{{Oh yeah, I remember the epiphany now. It was the idea that being a teacher is a radical form of generosity, and to be a good teacher, you have to first teach yourself. This applies perfectly to being a hitman. Being a good hitman is like giving the gift of death. The more you give out death, the more you become friends with death and an expert on death so when you deal it out, it's like a perfectly wrapped Christmas gift that your mark can accept, in a weird but perfectly understandable way. I'll have to write that down once this job is over.}}} Thinking relatively clearly, thinking fast, if you will, Darby pulled the trigger. BLAM, Coral's head was annihilated in a fuzzy red mist. The entire labyrinth was suddenly enfolded with a razor-sharp rococo foldedfoil of surveillance-tech, wrapping insect-size drones pouring out of orifices in the slatted skin like dirty smoke. With a sigh of satisfaction and a grunt of urgent momentum, Darb glanced at the bag of chips he wasn't eating. He suspected that he needed some kind of kevorkian telepathic sexual surgery. He was suddenly paralyzed, unable to decide whether to eat another chip or not to eat another chip, that was the question. He decided he wasn't hungry, but it took considerable struggle to reach that conclusion. Yep, he was STONED AGAIN. >_<

6.

𝕿runðling down the steps of the Potential Center's stairwell {99 flights}, he deftly changed into his "regular guy" disguise. Looking forward to plopping down, later, on his foamy bed and watching back-to-back episodes of *Seroquel Surgeons from Saturn*, his favourite show, he recalled how he had dragged his mattress into his spacious pink and gold bathroom the previous night in order to sleep adjacent to the toilet in the event of an incipient and/or sudden urge to vomit. He tried to remember if the mattress had been ruined by the vomit. Some of the social media exchanges he'd been having lately had really brought his anxiety levels to the paranoid freaking-out-point, but the angst was no match for his slick mantras, and deftly slipping on some brass knuckles, Darby systematically fought off a bunch of guards {{zero in, move out {{{fuckvortex}}} zero in, move out {{{suckvortex}}}}} who apparently knew he was the assassin, in a martial arts sequence, as elegantly as if it had been choreographed, like in a John Wick movie. It was hard to tell reality from fantasy at this point. Ever since he had started giving himself Indivisulen5™ injections, it was like a swarm of demons ran the computer that was his brain and he sloughed off like a puff of smoke, POOF. He'd blown his mind permanently. Broken it, as it were. He was a ruined individual, but that was what allowed him to be an unspeakably ruthless badass feared by everyone who knew what was good for them. The whole changeling myth, imposter syndrome, schizoid personality disorder, yadda yadda, he'd been through it all. He got into his fancy sportscar and began an extremely glamourous chase sequence with the cops. Addicted to fame and fashion and Instagram (and Vrumio, and Spune). A total celetoid idol. Grinning kawaii giving peace sign. Darby's car skids stylishly, spinning around 180 degrees, slick 3D graphix, drop-of-a-hat agile, batman badass. He flicks the ash off the end of his cigarillo as the awkward slapstick cops try to outmanœuvre him in an amorphous clown-car.

1.

We organize in more or less involuntary ways, like reflexive shopaholism, or spinal communism. The type of D+D session we do would be a total mindbreak for any average noob, if you will. I'm a damaged nerd with no life insurance; you'd better bear in mind there's probably no telling what I'll do next. Like in *Clifford (1994)*, the hilarious film in which Martin Short plays a bratty little kid whose psychotic immaturity makes the adults in charge of him completely miserable, or an advice video from subby influencers talking about the idea of "daddy issues" in a way that both romanticizes this semi-concept and acts like it's a legit scientific term or perhaps an academic notion worthy of Derridean deconstruction. Crashing the car, Darby runs through infested alleyscapes. Like *damn* if this isn't ruthlessly Sysyphean. Sissyphean. Which is the politically correct version? I forget. Fuck it. It's, you know, the gender neutral person who pushed a boulder up the hill, yadda, etc. It's Sssiphean. That's it, that's the gender neutral version. Sssiphean. And absurd. And on fire. And a state of exception. And a massive fucking emergency. "The fragmented shards of your former life decorate you like the bells of a comically tragic jester." Darby's schizophrenic mother had embroidered that phrase on a rustic throw-pillow as if it was of immense significance. I watch all of this from behind my dark sunglasses, my collar pulled up around my neck, and the end of rubber hosing tying off my arm clamped between my teeth so I can inject myself with Indivisulen5™ {I say this now sort of as the author of this récit but also partly as the protagonist, like his consciousness and mine are fused in a very clever, fictional way, a total lie, creative license if you will, a cheap trick, a sly inside joke but also a next-level string theory thing you gotta be a genius to get the gist of; idiots step aside, this is serious literature}.

I've become completely bored with sex. Naturally I was never really afraid of descending to the most fallen forms of fallenness, dark murky hellfrost, here in the complex_nested_ prison_spiral.exe, but it rapidly lost its novelty, especially as the microdrone_surveillancetech- nology made privacy a thing of the past, not to mention a tasteless faux pas. Darby got arrested so I'm just talking as me now. He got multiple life sentences.

I've exhausted the library now, and the shop- ping center is a vast waste of time, iterations of scripted dialogue looping back to uptight repetitiousness. Actually maybe I am still Darby but, like, just in his imagination or something. He kicks at a slimy seductress, half-rotted- through with weeping sores, rasping a stupid prophecy through her pointlessly pointed sybilline prosthetically lengthened teeth. "See a dentist," I blurt out, stupidly but also gruffly, caving her face in easily with a soft push, a push that gives me maniacal pleasure. Her face collapses like a decomposing pumpkin. Yikes. Frown frowns. I frown. You frown. We all frown. I'm Frown, I'm James, I'm Grendel, I'm zvrzh_G™. Who are you? *That's* the fucking question. *Who the fuck are you???* Okay, just kidding, sorry for the aggression, it's been a long day.

I had long since determined that the degenerate filth that decorated this fallen place were less than subhuman rabble and deserved to be in the most stressful slavery imaginable, like factory-farmed cattle strapped with robotic milk-extractors and forced to watch horrible child-oriented TV from the early days (1995-1998) of the famously smarmy Berlin-based channel *Nickelodeon*. After that they should be subjected to various forms of extreme torture, like water-boarding and Eminem records played at full blast like in Abu Ghraib. Inundated with ideology. Helplessly infantilized and alienated by all of this. Even gender grows devoid of meaning. I could only relate to them on the most intuitive, animalistic level, these slaves. With sex being off the table as a means of initiation, I was at a loss.

So I started to kill them out of pity. That's how I (the author) became an *actual* hitman. This part is 100% true. Either hitman or serial killer, I can't remember because I can't distinguish between externally issued directives and internal notions that are purely of my own devising. It's a form of schizophrenia. Either way, my morality is inconsistent. He (me, but now in the third person) picked the dirt from his fingernails, absent mindedly considering the possibility of clipping them. His optic chiasm buzzed with hyperaggressive vibes. He penetrated deeper into this train of thought and did more research, stopping to take notes and gaze profoundly into the distance like a genius of the romantic genre. He figured that this powerless paranoia didn't apply to him since he was a middle-class Jew whose ancestors had emigrated from Russia during WWI and thus it was only his great-grandfather's family who were Russian-Jewish-American immigrants, technically, even though this was never really a subject of discussion in his family, which was incredibly well assimilated. His estranged son Pablo, whose mother was the daughter of a family of

Portuguese immigrant workers, had received a fantastic education from the world's leading art schools and always seemed extremely disenchanted and surly. Pablo was a sculptor who liked working in bronze, for the most part. He'd sculpt Mickey Mouse's face but it would look all gooey and melted and shit, or he'd sculpt Donald Trump but his face would look all kawaii-like. Cool. Invisalign your life. In this particular video I'm talking about my experience of coming out as a lesbian. Having stayed up all night stoned, sitting a huddled mess like the R. Crumb drawing, having taken all sss medication. I really made a breakthrough today. I'm serious.

8.

Eee {nonbinary pronoun} was in a state of vague boredom that was turning hellish, even as eee felt the youtube algorithm honing in on mmm {object form of eee}, trying to convert mmm to a lifestyle vibe eee wasn't really into. Zero in and move. Polarizing mmm. Yes, this was the most boring boredom ever. It could be dangerous, even. Last night's bout of smoking weed left mmm feeling somewhat inspired, but had the inspiration worn off yet? True, eee had new goals for sss {possessive form of eee} work. But eee was slammed with inertia. Thrown back against the wall by entropy. Eee stared at the iridescent, reflective material of sss flip flops. Eee leaned sss head against the desk, bracing it with sss hands, the way eee used to do in elementary school when eee was bored and the teachers figured it was fine eee was just a gifted child it was okay for mmm to zone out sometimes. Eee flexed sss muscles, replaying the hit eee had done on Jessica Mimegnome the previous day, effortlessly snapping rrr neck, deft with purpose. Hide the body in a dumpster, no problem. Jessica was just a whore, nobody cared about rrr. 838K subscribers, 1M views 2 years ago. Stop trying to distract mmm. Ah yes, the old thinking is bad. The bible is the right thing. III get comments all time, it resonates with a lot people. Mmm Catholic school was uniquely terrible. Growing up being gay (or just, in general, growing up), 3.3K comments, only 126 thumbs down. 33K thumbs up. Ooh boy. This is interesting. Because now III'mmm wondering... Www weren't in our uniforms that day, III was wearing a tanktop. Mind you III'mmm like, a 12-year-old kid. Honestly, it didn't dawn on mmm that III was a child. III was mortified. Religious people and the indecency of bra straps is very much a thing. You know what III'mmm sayin'?

Hello friends, III'mmm looking extra goth mom today. III live in a high rise, but mmm neighbours... III'mmm definitely past mmm baby gay phase. But III think III still have that little baby gay self in the back of mmm brains. III'mmm very privileged to live in Toronto... III'mmm just bombarded with so much homosexuality... The dumbest discourse III've seen in a while. YYY could see the cracks in rrr gestures and those wild looks that asked why yyy were staring at rrr even though sss was obviously performing. Maybe sss had ADHD. III don't even know if yyy were actually LGBTQ.

9.

Straight is... neutral. Yyy're left out of Pride, it's for LGBTQ. Look my guy, it ain't that deep. This is garbage discourse. Tumblr. There are really straight people out there... My guy, do you have any respect for LGBTQ history at all??! It can seem like it's all just flamboyant fun, but there are places in the world where horrible things happen to people just because they're gay. Yyy don't need straight pride because it's always been okay for yyy to be straight. Jesus Christ yyy were such a good ally until yyy decided that yyy, a straight person, were the most important component of the gay community. Fuck that Heterosexual Pride Day nonsense. RRR curation of posts is good, III like it. III've gone from goth mom to just absolute gay trash kid. This trend made mmm a heterophobe.

Sadistic barbie, this is the bratty bottom anthem, change mmm mind. Femdoms rise for our national anthem. Gratitude is so powerful. It is the most wonderful feeling within when www experience it. Listen to this every day for 21 days. Remember to feel gratitude for all that yyy already have and all that yyy are in the process of manifesting. III had some dental surgery III needed to get done. So for today's video, Miley Cyrus dropped a new album. III have not listened to it at all. So III figured III would do another album review. III love doing these. III think yyy guys love when III do them. Please make sure yyy subscribe, yyy hit that like button, this album III was actually really excited for. III think what eee's doing right now is *so dope*. It definitely fits with stuff III like. That's something III want to talk about, weaponizing one's YouTube audience.

{{Blam!}}

{{{You Died}}}

{{Game Over}}

>_<

www.ingramcontent.com/pod-product-compliance
Lightning Source LLC
Chambersburg PA
CBHW071351130626
46556CB00005B/2137